This Chicken House book belongs to
That's Me!

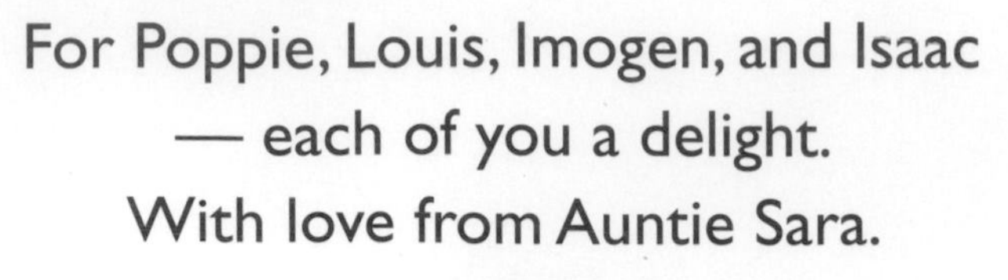

For Poppie, Louis, Imogen, and Isaac
— each of you a delight.
With love from Auntie Sara.
— S. S.

For all my favorite Sarahs.
— M. C.

A Note from Margaret Chamberlain About How She Created the Pictures in I'm Me!
"To start, I do a lot of drawings in pen and ink — the ordinary way, on ordinary paper. The magic begins when I scan these drawings into my computer. Using a tablet and stylus to add color and texture to the ones I like best, I have endless options to change and resize the images, create patterns, and have a lot of fun!"

ISBN 978-0-545-39979-1

 Published by Scholastic Inc. First published in the United Kingdom by Chicken House, 2 Palmer Street, Frome, Somerset BA11 1DS. CHICKEN HOUSE, SCHOLASTIC, and associated logos are trademarks and/or registered trademarks of Scholastic Inc.

12 11 10 9 8 7 6 5 4 12 13 14 15 16/0

Printed in the U.S.A. 40

First Scholastic paperback printing, October 2011

Body text was set in Gill Sans.
Display text was set in Countryhouse.
Book design by Whitney Lyle

I'm Me!

By

Sara Sheridan

Illustrated by

Margaret Chamberlain

Chicken House

SCHOLASTIC INC.

New York Toronto London Auckland
Sydney Mexico City New Delhi Hong Kong

"Peekaboo,
Auntie Sara.
It's me!"
"Peekaboo, Imogen!
Ready to have some fun?"

"yes,
yes,
yes, I am!
Can we play pretend?"

"Yes, yes, yes, we can!

Let's see. Will you be...

. . . a naughty monkey?
And I'm feeding you fruit on
a hot, sandy beach
in Zanzibar?

We'll swim with the dolphins
and splash in the waves
and swing from the trees
in the jungle."

"Oh, no!"
said Imogen.
"I'm not a smelly
monkey today.

Today I want to be..."

"...a beautiful princess!"

said Auntie Sara.
"We'll wear pretty, poufy ball gowns
and big, sparkly crowns. We'll ride
on white horses and dance
beneath the stars."

"No, thank you!"
said Imogen.
"I'm not some
silly princess.

Today I want to be..."

". . . a witch's kitty cat?"

said Auntie Sara.
"We can whizz like the wind
on a broomstick!

We'll stir secret potions in a bubbling black pot and cast spells with our magic wands. Meow!"

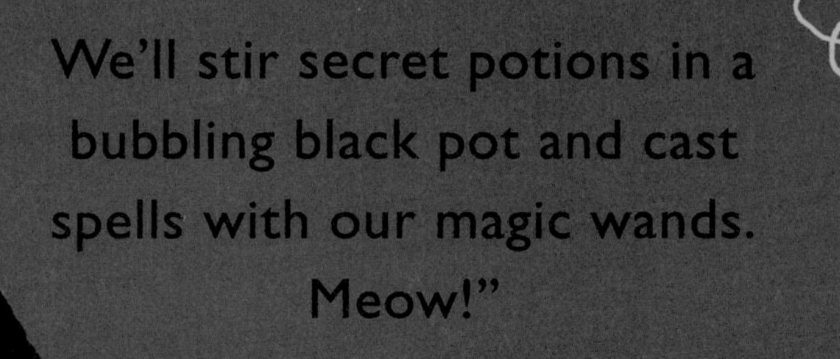

"No, not today," said Imogen. "I'm not a scratchy-clawed cat.

Today I want to be ..."

". . . a talking, squawking pirate's parrot!"

said Auntie Sara. "The scariest on the Seven Seas. Sit on my shoulder and we'll search the ocean blue for buried treasure chests!"

"I don't think so, not today,"

said Imogen. "I'm not a chatty parrot.

Today I want to be . . ."

said Auntie Sara.
"We'll teach them to swoop through hoops and loop-dee-loop,
and fly them high in the sky."

"A crazy
dragon tamer?"
said Imogen.
"Hmmm,
not today.
Today I want to be ..."

"...a far-out astronaut!" said Auntie Sara.

"And we're zooming through space, passing planets and stars, looking for aliens on Mars!"

"N-O No,"
said Imogen.
"I'm not an
astronaut.

Today I just
want to be . . .

. . . ME!"

"Oh, I see!"
said Auntie Sara.
"And what would YOU like
to do today?"

“Follow me!”
said Imogen.
“Let’s go outside. Let’s . . .

. . . go to the park and play on the swings!
We can see who goes the highest
and sings the loudest."

"I love the park!"
said Auntie Sara.
"Then what?"

"We'll jump to the
ground and toss a ball
around," said Imogen,
"till we're puffing
and we turn pink!

Or we could . . .

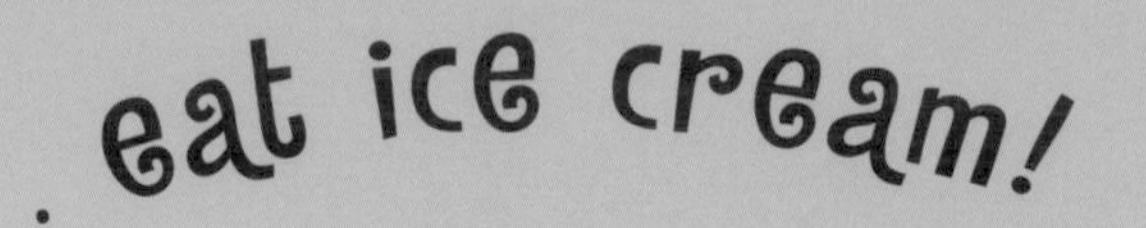

Mmm . . .
the stickiest, drippiest, yummiest cones,
the biggest we've ever seen!"

"Delicious!"
said Auntie Sara.
"And after that?"

"Maybe," said Imogen,
"we could . . .

. . . go back home. And we'll snuggle up **tight** for some stories about **witches** and **dragons** and **knights**!

Today, Auntie, what I want most of all is
for you to be you and me to be

ME!"

And Auntie Sara agreed.